In The Year 2020

Dani Quattrone

To my family and the loves of my life:
Matt, Lucas, Sofia and Nugget;
this book is not only inspired by you, **it is for you**.
May you remember this year as one filled
with silver linings, sweetness, love, gratitude,
and epic kitchen dance parties.

IN THE YEAR 2020,
there was a pandemic.

"What is that?" You ask?
Here, let me explain it.

A virus called Covid-19, got many sick.

And though it was tragic,
it MADE US ALL THINK...

Is there a way
to make our world better?

"It's time," we said,
"LET'S DO THIS TOGETHER."

What happened next, with PATIENCE and TIME...

A new and improved world,
started to SHINE.

This world was KINDER,
we all wore a mask.

An easy fix to the problem,
and a CONSIDERATE TASK.

This world was FRIENDLIER, EQUAL and DIVERSE.

We all lived in harmony,
OUR EARTH, our Universe!

This world was SWEETER,
COLORFUL and INCLUSIVE.

LOVE IS FOR EVERYONE,
hate and division are no excuses.

This world was HAPPIER,
we spent more time together.

We LAUGHED, DANCED, PLAYED
and got to know each other better.

This world was HEALTHIER,
we spent more time having FUN.

There's no need to hurry,
when we're out in the SUN.

This world was TASTIER,
we all learned to BAKE.

We GREW HOME GARDENS,
and celebrated with CAKE.

This world was CLEANER,
we restored Mother Nature.

Look at the HAPPY POLAR BEAR,
relaxing up in the glacier.

The sound of LAUGHTER,

the sight of TOGETHERNESS,

the taste of LOVE,

and the feeling of HOPE now fill up OUR world.

As you can see, sweet child of mine,
WHEN WE WORK TOGETHER
the outcome is truly divine.

First paperback edition 2020.

Illustrations by Ash Agnite.

ISBN: 979-8-6958-7182-1 (paperback)

www.buddhabellymama.com

Made in the USA
Columbia, SC
13 December 2020